For Jean Preece
—J.C.

For Dan
—L.M.

Library of Congress Cataloging-in-Publication Data:
Cole, Joanna. Don't call me names! / by Joanna Cole ; illustrated by Lynn Munsinger.   p.   cm. — (A Just right book) Summary: Nell is afraid of Mike and Joe because they always tease her and make fun of her, until the day she stands up to them on behalf of her friend Nicky. ISBN 0-679-80258-4 (trade). — ISBN 0-679-90258-9 (lib. bdg.) [1. Behavior—Fiction. 2. Friendship—Fiction.] I. Munsinger, Lynn, ill. II. Title. III. Series: Just right book (New York, N.Y.) PZ7.C67346Do 1990 [E] — dc20 89-35412 CIP AC

Manufactured in the United States of America   1 2 3 4 5 6 7 8 9 0

JUST RIGHT BOOKS is a trademark of Random House, Inc.

A Just Right Book

DON'T CALL ME NAMES!

By Joanna Cole • Illustrated by Lynn Munsinger

Random House 🏠 New York

Nell lived on Pond Street. She loved it there. The flat end of the street was good for softball. The hilly end was good for roller-skating. And the pond was terrific for swimming.

There were only two problems on Pond Street.
Mike and Joe. They always teased Nell.

Mike and Joe made fun of her name. They called,

"Nell, Nell, dumbbell!"

They made fun of her legs. They sang,

"Two sticks, toothpicks!"

They made Nell cry, and then they yelled,

"What's wrong, Hop-along?"

Nell ran home, and Mike and Joe ran after her, shouting,

"Nell's as green as a lima bean!"

"Don't cry, Nell," said a small, shy voice.

It was Nicky, the new kid on the block. He was peeking out from behind his house.

"I *like* green," he said, and then he ran away.

Nicky made Nell feel better, even if he was too shy to stay.

The next day Amy came over to Nell's house. Amy was the opposite of shy!

"Can you play, Nell?" shouted Amy.

"Sure. Come in," said Nell. She wanted to play indoors. Mike and Joe could not tease her there.

First, Amy and Nell played dress-up.
"Let's play outside now," said Amy.
"Later," said Nell.

Next they made a big city with blocks.

"Let's go out now," said Amy.

"Later," said Nell.

So they baked cookies. Amy ate most of them. Then she said, "Let's go roller-skating."

"Later," said Nell.

"It *is* later!" said Amy, and she pushed Nell out the door.

Nell saw the green grass. She saw the blue sky. She saw Nicky waving from his tree house. Then she saw Mike and Joe.

"Quick, hide!" Nell gasped. She pulled Amy behind a tree and she hid behind another one.

Nell and Amy were very quiet. Then Amy said in a loud voice, "Why are we hiding?"

"Shhh! They will hear you," whispered Nell.
"*Who* will hear me?" called Amy.
"Mike and Joe," hissed Nell.
"Oh, *them*," said Amy loudly. "I'm not afraid of *them*."

Amy ran out from behind the tree.

When Mike saw Amy, he made fun of her quills.

"Hey, pincushion!" he yelled. "How does your mother hug you—*carefully*?"

"Run away, Amy!" called Nell, but Amy didn't run.

She looked right at Mike and said,

"I'm rubber, and you're glue.
It bounces off me and sticks to you!"

And she tossed her head.

Mike and Joe looked at each other. This never happened when they teased Nell.

"Amy is no fun," said Mike.

"Let's go ride our bikes," said Joe, and off they went.

When Mike and Joe were gone, Nell peeked out from behind the tree.

"Wow, Amy! You're really brave!" she said.

"Oh, you don't have to be brave to stand up to Mike and Joe," said Amy. "They just talk, and *I* can talk too. Now let's skate!"

Nell and Amy skated all afternoon. Mike and Joe did not bother them. Then Amy had to go home for supper.

"Bye, Nell," said Amy as she skated off. "See you tomorrow!" Nell skated home slowly by herself.

Mike and Joe biked by again. They saw that Nell was alone.
They rode up quietly behind her. "Watch out!" they yelled.

Nell jumped. She lost her balance and fell down.

Mike and Joe started talking in high, sweet voices.

"Oooh! Oooh! Did the little froggy fall down?" squeaked
Joe as if he were talking to a baby.

Mike answered in the same voice, "Oh, I hope she didn't
hurt herself!"

Nell's knee did hurt, and she started to cry.

"Crybaby," said Mike, laughing.

Nell took off her skates and ran. Mike and Joe chased her all the way back to her house. She went inside and slammed the door.

"I'm never going out again," Nell said to herself. "Never!"

The next day Amy came over.
"Nell! Nell! Come outside and look!" she called.
Nell peeked out. On every tree was a sign that said:

COSTUME PARADE! PRIZES!
Dress up and come to Pond Park Saturday!

"I'm going to be a princess," said Amy. "What will you be?"
"I'm not sure I can go on Saturday," Nell told her.

Nell spent the whole day thinking.
She really wanted to go to the Costume
Parade, but she was scared. If only she
could come up with a costume Mike and
Joe couldn't make fun of.

"Maybe I'll be a karate kid," she thought. Then she decided that Mike and Joe would probably say something like,

"Is that a karate chop,
Or a karate *hop*?"

She decided to dress as a ballerina, but she was afraid Mike and Joe might say,

"Do a dance, do a dance,
So we can see your underpants!"

Dressing up like a cucumber or a tomato would be funny, Nell thought. But she was sure Mike and Joe would say something like,

"We HATE vegetables!!!"

And then they would pretend to be sick to their stomachs.

Nell was ready to forget about going to the Costume Parade when she had another idea. What if she made a giant monster costume? Mike and Joe would never know the monster was Nell.

Nell worked hard on the costume, and by Saturday it was ready.

She put it on, opened the door, and started walking
toward Pond Park. Up ahead a tiny figure was skipping along.
It was Nicky, dressed as an astronaut. He looked very proud
of himself.

At the edge of Pond Park, Nell saw a beautiful princess—it was Amy. Under a tree stood a cowboy and a pirate—Joe and Mike. Uh-oh! But Mike and Joe paid no attention to the monster.

They were too busy pointing at Nicky and laughing.
"Look, it's a moon man," said Joe. Then he called,

"One look at your face
And I know you're from space!"

Nicky stopped skipping and frowned.
"Have you ever seen such a *small* astronaut, Joe?" said
Mike. Then he turned to Nicky and said,

"I'll ask you a riddle.
How come you're so little?"

Mike and Joe were spoiling Costume Day for Nicky. It was mean to make fun of Nicky's size. Nell was so angry she forgot to be scared. She walked right up to Mike and Joe.

Mike saw the giant monster coming toward him.

"Stop picking on Nicky!" a strange voice growled from inside.

"Make me, monster-face!" said Mike. His voice sounded a little shaky. "Oh, look! There's my friend Pete. I think I'll say hello to him." And Mike took off.

The monster took another step closer and towered over Joe.
"Stop calling names—or else!" said the monster.
"Wait for me, Mike!" yelled Joe, and he ran too.
Nell watched them go hide behind a tree.
"How about that?" she said in a surprised voice. "*They*
were afraid of *me!*"

"Nell, is that you in there?" asked Nicky.
"Wow, Nell, that's a great costume!" said Amy.

Amy, Nicky, and Nell all got prizes. Amy's prize was a red kite for the Most Beautiful costume. Nicky won a blue kite for the Most Spaced-Out costume. And Nell won a yellow kite for the Scariest costume.

Mike and Joe didn't win a prize. They stayed behind the tree, and the judges didn't see them.

Afterward, Nell felt hot inside her costume, so she took it off.
"Hey, the monster was Nell!" Joe said to Mike.
Then they both started laughing and shouted,

"Nell, Nell, dumbbell!"

"That monster wasn't anything to be afraid of at all!" Mike said.
Nell knew they were right—the monster wasn't really scary.
But their words weren't really scary either. Nell shouted back,
"I am *not* a dumbbell. And what *you* say is what *you* are."

Then Nell tossed her head, just the way Amy did.
Mike and Joe stopped short. They looked at Nell. They
looked at each other.
"This is no fun," said Joe.
"Let's go," said Mike.

Then Nell, Amy, and Nicky had a wonderful afternoon
flying their kites.